Jonathan's Children

By B. C. Moore

Jonathan's Children

ISBN-13: 978-1475266580

First Edition

© Text B. C. Moore 2012

The right of B. C. Moore to be identified as the author of this work has been asserted in accordance with Sections 77 and 78 of the Copyright, Designs and Patents Act 1988.

First published in 2012

A Cataloging-in-Publication (CIP) record of this book is held at the British Library and at the Library of Congress.

SYNOPSIS

Tenants living on the banks of the Mersey once spoke humorously of their `non-paying guests`. Small children, animals seen mostly out the corner of the eye, a shadow on the stairs. Then slowly it changed. Not so funny now, their whimpering and scampering about in the dead of the night. The elderly shivered in their beds, they pulled the sheets to cover their face, as they watched the shadowy children, they glared back, with gaunt faces, hardly human. 'Lost souls' the old folk whispered, as they crossed themselves.

The hauntings became omens, always followed by terrible events. The tenant's children were out of control, wicked and angry. The young men in particular fell into deep depressions, unable to cope with the sightings and sounds when they were alone. They felt unable to confide, who would believe them? Where had they come from? Why had they attached themselves to the riverside dwellings? Who was Jonathan? They heard his name called eerily in the darkness by a young girl. What part of history had landlocked them? Or had they always been there? If the tenants had known the battle that was going on to capture their children's spirits, they would have fled as far as they could from the murky, haunted waters of the river.

JONATHAN'S CHILDREN

The year was 1738, England's rich were getting wealthier, the masses desolate. Merchants in the north in particular were thriving. Their sailing ships trading from the small quayside on the shores of the Mersey. The land workers living in the sleepy hamlets and farms that surrounded the bay, made arduous journeys in their horse drawn carts to the shoreline to barter their wares. Soon, large wooden sheds sprung up to house the many goods and foodstuffs. Living became harder on the land, the poor weather all but decimating the crops. The starved, rustic population thronged to live and work by the river. The Masters lived there too in their fine mansions. The divide between the rich and poor was never greater.

Ester lay dying on the flea ridden sacking on the dirt floor of a freezing wooden shack. It was amidst the now overgrown fields she had worked for all forty years of her life. Now she looked twice her age. The owner, her Master, had succumbed to an invader from a far off land. More vicious than the Vikings or Romans, more callous than the Normans. None could compare to the black rat! Hidden and brought in by the sailing ships. Its deadly cargo, the flea, swollen with the blood of Bubonic plague victims. It struck the densely populated quayside first. Then it was carried in the sacks of flour by the farmers to the isolated, rural hamlets and farms. Its effects were devastating and unknown to the peasants. They tried treating it with all manner of potions, to no avail. The merchants and the wealthy landowners quickly left their homes on the banks of the river. They blamed the filthy sewage floating on the river for the fever now known as the Black Death! They built and lived in their magnificent houses, high on the hill. The riverside was like a ghost town, with its walking dead! It was eerie in the day as well as the night. It was populated only by the bereft and sick unfortunates who could not afford to leave. Whole families were isolated and died, their decaying bodies left to decompose or thrown into the river that was once their lifeline. The wealthy, concerned only that their workforce was diminishing. The news from the rest of England was even worse; it would seem that almost a third of the population had succumbed to the plague.

Ester stirred. Once pretty, her face was hollow. Her long, black hair lay lank and wet with sweat. Her big blue eyes that once twinkled with the joy her five children gave her, were dull and for the most time, unseeing. She tried, with the last of her breath, to urge her family to leave. Make their way to the quayside, where they might stand a chance. Surely someone would help? Maybe the church, after all soon they would be orphans. Almost fourteen, Jonathan was her eldest. A quiet, conscientious boy; he was wise beyond his age. Born to the land, children matured quickly, expected to contribute their labour almost as soon as they could walk. He had been tall and sturdy for his age, with his mother's blue eyes and his father's straw coloured hair. Life had been hard, especially in the winter, but at the end of a long day, or after a good harvest, he got his reward. All the family, sitting around the big wooden table he had helped his father to build. The ruddy faces of his siblings, happy and healthy. Their home was a small holding, owned by a big land owner. Compared to most, he was a generous, God fearing man. Esters family had always lived in and served him in the big house. When she married, he allowed her to build on his property and work the land. He accepted their produce in return for rent. Jonathan looked down at his dying mother, knowing how this nightmare had begun. Last year's crops had failed miserably. His father was forced to find work on the quay side. He would return with what flour and grain he could afford to buy with his pittance of a wage as a dock labourer.

All that was at an end, it had all been in vain. Tears slipped down Esters face, she had not felt her new born, who had been suckling at her breast, stir for a long time. Jonathan showed no emotion, just steadfastly refused her weak pleas for him to leave her side. Now he reached down and gently removed the dead baby from her poisonous breast. Her sunken eyes rolled as she fought to stay conscious. Dry sobs wracked her as she looked into the gaunt faces of her children. They hovered around her like shivering scarecrows. The black rat watched warily from its nest of young in its hiding place in the rafters, its red, beady eyes glistening.

Ester knew it was time, already her dead family gathered at the foot of her straw bed. They called to her to 'let go!' She longed to be free of her sick body but she cried for her children. Her late husband waited, his face grim, knowing it was him who had carried the rat to his farm in the sack of flour. He too wanted his wife to be rid of her diseased body. Like her, he could find no peace in death, desolate at leaving his children, although he knew they would not be long in following. She was slipping fast. 'Go' she mouthed to Jonathan. 'Take them to the riverside where there are people who will help. I will meet you there when I have rested.' He could hardly hear her. She prayed he would take them, she pleaded with her dull eyes.

Only now he relented, she had `that look`. He had seen it many times, his grandparents, aunts, uncles, his father. He had no tears left to shed for her, just a heavy ache in his heart. Soon she would be gone too. He would go now, while there was still some light on this bitterly cold December afternoon. The journey would take at least two days and nights on foot. He pulled at his two brothers, James just turned eleven and Michal seven. Then there was his baby sister, Emma. Just three, she was no longer the chubby toddler of latter months. The children looked mournfully at their mother. They feared she had already left them; her eyes no longer followed them as they reluctantly struggled out into the bitter cold wind.

It was a grey, stark winters day. 'Strange', he thought, as they struggled painfully slow along icy country paths, hunched against the wind. He was surprised to see others in the half light. They too were battling along. He thought they would be alone on the lanes. It had been so long since he had seen anyone other than his family. But there were many, all heading for the bay. Some stopped by the frozen streams, They lit fires to heat up their watery broths. Most were like themselves, groups of solitary children. Frozen, in their scant clothing, many with rags tied around their feet. Some, who looked at deaths door, had bare feet. For the first time in weeks, just when he thought he would never cry again, tears burnt his eyes. Not for himself, but for the desperate plight of these children.

'Dear God.' He prayed. 'Have mercy on us.'

He managed, after many hours in the dark fields, to snare a small rabbit. The brothers cried, not wanting to wait for it to cook properly. They pulled at it like a pack of dogs, cold blood congealed around their filthy mouths. With hardly any flesh, it served only to increase their hunger, except for Emma, who ate just a tiny morsel, and then only to please her beloved Jonathan.

Some of the travellers told them tales of the quayside and town, they said it was overrun with big, fat, edible rats. Their initial feelings of nausea were quickly suppressed when they were informed they tasted `just like chicken`. It spurred them on; the river could be seen now in the frosty distance. It was then they heard the plaintive cries of a small girl. She sat by the hedge, dressed only in a thin, dirty, grey smock dress that reached her bare feet. Emma ran to her, they looked to be the same age. They forgot their own extreme situation in a bid to comfort the little waif. In between sobs that tore at his heart, she told them her name was Hannah. She had become parted from her mother when they had been evicted from their shelter. She said it was because her father had the fever and would not awaken when her mother shook him. Jonathan nodded knowingly. He knew people were terrified to come near you; it was felt this plague could be passed simply by touch! Hannah seemed to be feeling a little cheerier, holding Emma's hand, they trundled along. It seemed her company had lifted his sister's spirits; she was acting like a little mother to Hannah.

It was rapidly growing dark, the snow and heavy clouds blotted out any light from the full moon. As they neared the river, two brothers, who looked to be the same age as James and Michal, stopped them. Their faces and bodies were skeletal, their clothes just tatters, worse even than their own. The eldest said he was Jack, his younger brother, John. They told a horrendous tale. They had both been desperately sick. Their parents told them they would go and get help. They were locked in the cellar. Many days past, they never returned! Their fevers finally broke and to their relief, one morning, the door was ajar, they offered no reason for this. They gave a tearful description of their parents.

Jonathan shook his head sadly. 'No' he told them, he had not seen them. Their soulful eyes prompted him to suggest they join their group. They brightened up and walked beside his brothers, they too seemed cheered by their company. Jonathan fell quiet; things were so much worse than his isolated family had feared. This fever seemed to have spread everywhere. He feared for them all! What lay ahead of them? Soon they neared some small hamlets, but there was no food to be found. They scavenged what they could from neglected fields of winter vegetables. Too soon, a band of ragged people ran out from the small shelters, armed with clubs they chased them away. Jonathan guessed they were fearful of catching the fever from them. They met more and more deserted children, they too begged to be allowed to join them. Jonathan could not find it in his heart to refuse them!

As they travelled along, they each spoke in small, pitiful voices. All had a horror story to tell! Parents who had died or left them to find help. One way or another, they were all abandoned! None had a parent!

They started to flag, the cold and hunger making them wail. He drove then on relentlessly, with promises of food and shelter 'yes', he told the crying infants, 'your mammas will be there.'

He was amazed at how many of them there were now, two gross or more he guessed. Some could hardly walk, but even when left behind, something, he could do nothing about, 'there was just too many,' somehow, they would re-join them at the next camp. As he neared the river, he feared his mother had been mistaken to send them this way. It had taken them longer than he had anticipated, two horrendous days and nights! Finally, when the moon was high, they made a rough shelter of sorts on the grey, wet sands of the Mersey. It was sheltered by the sand dunes near to the water's edge. They hid away from the angry towns people; he feared they would kill them. They huddled together for warmth. He looked around at the swirling mist, it was dusk. He could see no adults, just hoards of deserted, half dead, ragged children! He did not know how they still lived! They all wandered over to him, staring into the flames. They all pleaded to be allowed to stay with him; Jonathan hung his head with the disparity of it all.

'We have nothing' he said simply.

The children looked around fearfully 'we just want to be with you.' They cried.

He understood, he moved over. They spent their first night by the water. These children too told their stories. They sobbed, broken hearted, when they spoke of their parents, who had somehow left them behind. It was so cold most of the children could not rest; they became restless and wandered off into the night. Jonathan held his brothers and sister, trying to keep them warm; gradually they drifted in and out of sleep. The other children returned at dawn, still they could not settle. They roamed around aimlessly.

Jonathan was sick, feverous! He struggled to open his burning eyes. He looked to the river, it was heavy with fog, the bells on the buoy clanged, creating a weird atmosphere. He flayed about, fighting the illness with what little strength he had left. He could not succumb to this fever! His family needed him! He turned to his sleeping brothers, so alike, almost like twins, as he was fair, they were dark. Emma's blonde curls were dirty and matted, her blue eyes closed, her hollow, almost translucent cheeks like marble with the cold. He fell into a deep well of despair; there was nothing he could do! He kept slipping into darkness, the children awoke, they were distraught when they could not rouse him. Emma clung to him, her painfully thin arms wrapped around his neck. She called his name pitifully, over and over! He fought in vain to get out of this nightmare, stay awake! Only the `clang` of the fog bells gave him some comfort, telling him he was still in the land of the living!

The bells had silenced, he opened his eyes, it was dawn. The fog was lifting off the river, clinging, only in parts, to the sands. The water was low, exposing the grey, desolate sands. Small, ragged children wandered along, searching for shellfish or anything edible amongst the rocks. Some groups ran to the nearby grain sheds and flourmill. They hoped to get there before the bedraggled workforce arrived. Once there, they searched for rats, pigeons. His brothers and sister huddled into to him, Emma had drifted back to sleep, be it somewhat fitful. Then he heard it! He was not sure, could not believe, he strained to hear. There, again! He sat up; it was coming from the water's edge. The sun was bouncing weakly from the murky water. There were still patches of mist on the sands, but he recognised her! There was no doubt! His eyes grew wide, she was dressed as last he had seen her on her deathbed, in a long, black dress. She looked bewildered, lost, distraught! His heart went out to her. He struggled to get to his feet.

'Jonathan' her voice was getting weaker.

'Mamma!' He called to her as he stumbled across the sands toward her, gaining strength as he got nearer. She could not see him because of the mist, but he could clearly see her. He kept calling to her but his voice was drowned by the sound of the water. Throwing caution to the wind, he waved wildly. 'Mamma' this time she stopped! She half turned, her face lifted upward. His heart leapt, a sob strangled in his throat, she heard! 'Mamma!' His legs were stronger; he urged them to go faster! It was hard in the wet sand, but he was gaining, he knew she would hear. Suddenly he felt small, grabbing hands tearing at his arms and legs. He was being dragged backwards, almost to the ground! He fought back, desperate to be free! He could not understand what was happening! He saw and recognised them; it was the children he had left at dawn. They tore at him, their faces grim, determined, full of anger! 'No, Jonathan!' They screamed. Pleading, 'You must come back!' Their usually lifeless eyes were bright with tears. 'You must return! Emma is dying! She calls out for you! She has the fever!'

He stopped, remembering how ill she looked when last he saw her. He put his head in his hands, he was in turmoil.

Somehow, his mother had survived; she was out there, searching for them. He watched in utter despair, she was heading to where the sand was exposed, the water low, to the other side. He screamed after her. 'No! No!' She didn't hear, he renewed his efforts to be free but they clung to him.

'She will be back.' They cried. 'Your sister needs you.'

He knew they were right, he had to go back, his mother would return. He could see her fading in the mist, he had to believe she would be back, Emma needed him. Tears stung his eyes. He turned back into the fog, but now he was glad, he could see Emma, her little arms outstretched, staggering around in the mist. She was crying out for him, he ran to her and held her close.

'Jonathan!' She sobbed. 'I was so ill I was on fire. I was crying for you!'

He touched her brow, it was cool. He soothed her. 'The fever has broken, you will be well now, we both will,' For the first time, he believed it. He did feel stronger; maybe they would survive after all. He looked around, 'Where are Peter and James?'

She shook her head. 'They must be looking for you.'

Many terrible days and nights of searching followed. He was frantic with worry, his brothers were lost! He had not seen his mother again; his only hope was that they had found each other. 'Yes.' He comforted himself. 'That is what has happened; they are on the other side of the river, at the next low tide they will return.'

NEW ABODE

Things had gotten a little better for the children, while out searching for his brothers; Jonathan had found a more permanent shelter for his growing band. They moved into an abandoned house on the waterfront. They were safe, as long as they stayed out of sight in the daylight; more important to Jonathan, it provided some shelter from the elements. He was happy with its proximity to the riverside and sands. He needed to be near to the water so he could keep searching for his family.

The two brothers he had befriended at the beginning of their travels, stayed by his side. They helped ease his loss, even making him laugh with their pranks. They would creep around outside in the darkness, wailing into the wind. When some vagrant happened upon their shelter, they would creep around him howling. Terrified, their unwanted guest would run screaming, of `ghouls!` Then there were the other times, he felt they went too far. He feared for the very life of a lone sea-fearer. Worse for drink, he was lost and swaying in the strong wind. He somehow sighted Jake, the elder brother, and called to him for directions. The two ran around him, shouting, pulling and pushing him to the water's edge. He tried to chase the tormenting Jake, calling him a demon! His younger brother Micheal took up the gauntlet. In the blink of an eye, he pushed the traumatised man into the stormy water, but for the speedy intervention of Jonathan fishing him out, he would have surely drowned! The brothers skulked about for days. They could not understand why the usually placid Jonathan had frowned and waved his finger at them. Jonathan feared that as well as the brothers, lots of the other children were becoming meddlesome. Their expressions always angry, frustrated! He feared for their very souls if their parents did not come for them soon. They were fast becoming out of control.

While out later that day, he went onto the sands in his nightly search for his family. The shoreline was crowded with the children. Suddenly he saw a woman; she cradled a new born baby. His heart leapt, until he realised it was not his mother, yet she seemed to recognise him. She smiled with relief and rushed toward him.

'Is it Jonathan? The friend of the lost children'

He was taken aback, not sure she meant him, he wondered at the description. Who was she?

She called to him again; she saw the look of puzzlement. 'Do not be feared, 'tis my little girl I am looking for, I cannot go over 'till I know for sure she is not here.' He was silent, at a loss as to how she knew his name. She seemed to know his thoughts, she smiled. 'Everyone speaks of you, how you look out for the children.'

Although surprised at what she said, he understood her plight, he just hoped he could help. He spoke softly. 'Your girl, what is her name?'

Her eyes became moist with emotion. 'Hannah' she whispered 'she was just three, I only left her to get help.' She looked down at the whimpering baby. 'Soon' she soothed.

Jonathan knew it had to be the same child they had befriended. He had come to believe, with the passage of time, her mother was surely lost to her. He was happy for them both, but sad for his sister. They had formed a fierce bond; Emma was very protective of her, but he knew what had to be done. 'I think I know of her.' He beckoned to the woman to follow him.

Her smile was reward enough; she was radiant as she followed. 'Thank you, may God bless you.' She said over and over.

As they neared the group of children, Jonathan was shocked to see some of the older children come running toward them. They were screaming obscenities! Screaming! Demented! She pulled back, clutching her baby to her, afraid! He stood before her, his hands rose in protest. 'What is this?' He protested. 'This is Hannah's mother; she has been searching for her for many months'.

The woman found her voice. 'Not months, many years.'

He thought he misheard, suddenly Hannah appeared, her eyes wide and bright, she held out her little arms. Her mother cried out with joy. Hannah ran toward her. The children went crazy! They ran in front of her, wailing screeching! The noise was horrendous! Once again, he had to fend them off.

The woman grabbed her girl's hand and they ran to the part of the water where it was low enough to cross. She called to him before running across to the other side. 'Goodbye Jonathan, God be with you until you find your mother.'

He did not have time to ponder her knowledge of him. The children were distraught, he could not understand their grief, he tried to calm them but they stormed off. One girl his age screamed at him. 'You should have hidden her! Soon we will have no one!'

He sat on his own, his head in his hands, except for Emma, who sobbed at the loss of her friend. He held her close and tried to comfort her, explain why she had to go. Her eyes welled with tears; she asked him why she could not go with them. He shook his head 'We have to wait for our mother, what she would think if she came back and we were not here?'. She quietened, but he saw a flash of anger in her lowered eyes and knew she still blamed him.

He tried to clear his thoughts. Of late his head had been like the weather, constantly foggy. 'What is wrong with everyone? Why is everyone changing so?' He thought back to last night on the sands. He had been unable to rest and they had all headed for the dunes, where they lay together. He had finally succumbed to a restless sleep. When he awoke, they were all strewn with wet seaweed brought in by the giant waves. When he had looked around he saw many new faces. Small children were waking, rubbing their eyes, as if from a deep, deep, sleep. He could only think they had arrived in the dead of the night. He also wandered that none asked for food anymore, then realised, he too had lost his appetite; it had all but diminished since his fever. He frowned, none of them ate anymore! They just wet their lips. He tried to remember when he had last seen them eat. He realised, with shock, he never had! They went out for hours, only returning to the sands when the water was on the ebb. They would say they had hunted and ate their fill, he could think no more! He took Emma by the hand; they left the dunes and walked slowly along the sands. He was hoping to be rid of the questions that had no answers, from his tangled thoughts. As he looked along the water's edge he was amazed to see a group of black children walking toward them. He knew only of their race from his bible teachings. They waved and walked quickly toward him. The group were attired in strange, colourful, robes; some of the older boys had deep markings on their cheeks. He knew they were from a far off land, yet when they spoke he understood, he did not think to question this. They numbered seven; the eldest, a boy of about fifteen years, led them. They asked if they could walk a while with them, he was more than happy with their company. As they did, they told terrible tales of kidnap and slavery. They had been taken forcibly from their villages in a land they called Africa. Their new Master had transported them in huge sailing ships; he put them deep in its bowels, with hardly enough water or food to keep them alive. Most had become desperately ill; those that died were thrown over the side. One small boy, who went by the name of Toby, showed him a deep scar on his back. He said this was caused by a giant fish, but for one of the black sailors fishing him out, he would have been eaten for sure. Jonathan's eyes were wide with shock. They told terrible stories of their people being taken to a land they called the America's. Once there, they were sold as slaves by the Merchants of the port they were now in. They had only escaped this by stowing away in the ship until it sailed back.

'I have never heard of such things.' He puzzled. They asked if they could stay with him, he sighed. 'I do not have anything.'

They shook their heads. 'We will ask for nothing, just your company.'

And so his band swelled some more, much to the delight of the others, who on their return from their wanderings, told of strange happenings ashore. Since their sleep last night in the high tide, there had been many changes, they declared. No one was sick with the Black Death! There were many strange buildings, the shoreline was hustling and bustling. The quay had become extended to accommodate the many sailing vessels, so stopping the water becoming low, in what they called a dock.

Jonathan felt fearful, how had this happened? The sands were a great part of their lives; they were ignored by the town's people. Where could they go if this continued? He covered his face with his hands in disbelief and despair? What was happening? How could all these changes happen during one night? He looked up to the shoreline to where their shelter should be, his mouth dropped open, it had gone! He spied hoards of children, some calm looking, some like them when they had first arrived, lost, bewildered. The latter were dressed in strange clothes. They wore foot-wear that he had never seen before. His head swam, he had no answers, he only knew it had something to do with the high tide. Another frightening thought flew to mind. All these changes, he fretted, how will my mother and brothers find me?

Overnight, the shoreline had shrunk! Great slabs of concrete covered their sands. He was frantic with worry, where it was all going to end!? He took Emma's hand and left the jabbering throng. He walked slowly, trying to clear his muddled thoughts. .

'Who are you? 'A man's deep voice, strong and vibrant filled the air. It was also right alongside of him, he jumped with the shock. The moon was high and full but he could see nothing through the sea mist that had suddenly descended. 'Can you hear me?' The voice boomed again.

Jonathan looked about, terrified. 'Who are you?' He shouted.

'So you do hear me!' The voice shouted back.

Jonathan stumbled backwards. 'Of course I can hear you, you are bellowing down my ear! Where are you!? I can not see you?'

The thunderous voice seemed even closer, 'I am searching for Toby.' He shouted, ignoring his question. 'Do you know of him?'

Emma had started to sob with fear; Jonathan pulled her to him, 'Stop shouting!' He demanded. ' you are frightening my sister.' He sensed someone very near.

'Are you still there?' The voice boomed again.

Emma was howling now, Jonathan covered his ears. 'I know him, I know of Toby!' He called in desperation. 'I will get him, now will you stop shouting? 'The voice had silenced, He looked around with still no clue to its source.

'Tell him it's his Papa' the voice said softly. 'I have come for him; I will take him to his Mama across the river.'

Jonathan's eyes searched along the sand, he could see the group of African children. They were begging the seafarers to be let on board the ship that was bound for their home land. The old salts, as usual, ignored their pleas.

Jonathan called out to them. 'Toby!' The boy turned, he had heard, he hurried toward him. 'Your Papa is here.' Jonathan shouted. The boy screamed with joy. The other children heard too and chased behind him. They pleaded with the boy. 'No! Do not go! Stay with us!'

Now Jonathan could see owner of the voice, a mountain of a man in startling red and gold robes that touched his bare feet. He smiled broadly, his arms outstretched, his eyes moist with happiness. Jonathan saw the children's looks of rage and hatred, as they chased after Toby. More and more children joined them. Jonathan knew their intent.

The man seemed unaware of them; he scooped the boy up into his arms. 'My boy!' He cried. 'All this time and you are still but a child.'

Jonathan threw himself in front of the pair; he did not have time to ponder upon his words. The children pulled and clawed at Tobies feet, weeping in despair. 'No! Toby does not leave us!'

The boy looked down at the crying children; he was torn between his joy at finding his father, and his bond with them. 'I must' he whimpered.

His father turned to the exposed sand that led across the water, the child threw his arms around his neck and clung tightly. Before they disappeared into the river mist, he turned to Jonathan. 'You, boy! You have been truly blessed, now you must find their parents too.'

The children tore at their faces in despair. They turned on Jonathan. 'Why?' They screamed, over and over. He stared at in shock and disbelief, He shouted over the noise. 'You know why! I have told you before! His father came for him.'

One of the older girls, whose parents had left her locked in a smoke filled house, pushed herself forward. She stood before him, her face almost touching his, growling into his startled face. Her eyes slanted, her usually pretty face, ugly and twisted with fury. 'Your mother came for you but you never left.' She snarled

He was at a loss at her anger, afraid of the physical change in her face. He stammered with fear. 'But you know why I never left! Emma needed me. My mother will return with my brother's.'

A hush descended, their expressions of hatred turned to pleasure. The two boys, who he had first befriended, pushed forward. The children faces grew excited, they now went by the name of `the skeletal brothers` The elder smiled slyly at him. 'She will never come back!' He swept his hand across the crowds. 'We can never leave! No-one will ever come looking for us. But you! You had your chance and missed it!' He looked across the rising water and then back to a white faced Jonathan. He threw his bony head back and laughed. 'You are trapped, like us!' They all joined in, laughing and laughing, pointing at him, dancing up and down with glee.

Jonathan felt his heart turn to lead. He was overcome with an unexplainable dread. Somehow, he knew what they said was true. He fought against it. 'I can follow when the water is low.' His head thundered. 'How can I be trapped?' He shouted 'I can swim across, look!' They all squealed with excitement as he ran towards the rising tide. He started to wade into the water, toward the opposite bank.

'Look down.' They shouted.

He looked, and was so overcome, he fainted away. Below the water, he did not exist!

'Like us!' They said in unison. They joined hands and danced around his half submerged body. Through a haze he looked up at them. They formed a giant circle, 'looking', he thought, trembling, 'like an old, faded picture'. They wailed, in high, thin voices, a haunting verse

'We are children of the tide'

'Under the water, we do hide.'

'Calling-----Calling.' Their high tones carried eerily on the wind.

Emma watched, her eyes lighting up. She ignored her brothers anguish. 'Me!' She pleaded, holding out her hands. They swung her around and around, her head fell back, her eyes closed. Jonathan saw it all as if in a terrible nightmare. He held his head in his hands; it was all becoming terribly clear. Time, as he once knew it, no longer existed, he was no longer in the land of the living. None of them were! Now he understood, it broke his heart, a sob caught in his throat. The only escape was if a loved one took you across. They were right, for most of

them this would not happen. How many centuries had
come and gone with the high tide? He did know one thing;
he would never accept that there was no hope.

WORLD WARS UNDER THE HIGH TIDE

Over the following years he re-united many of `Jonathans children`, as there band was now called. The living who had second sight, knew of them, they could see the shadowy figure of a lone boy surrounded by waifs and strays. Jonathan stayed close to the waterside, away from the skeletal brothers and their hoards of animalistic followers. They were vicious; they went searching, in packs, for lost children. Some, who had claimed a child's soul, were distraught when Jonathan stole them back and re-united them. Incensed at their loss, they would go into fierce rages in the nearby area, where they would lure a lone child to the water. Once in the water, they held them under and captured their soul. Jonathan had heard of this practise and he fought day and night to stop them. He kept the newly arrived close to him on the sands, in the hope their departed family would come for them. Of late there had been so many, he was becoming weary and disillusioned... There were times when he dwelled on how the children had trapped him, and then he too would rage, He could see the time fast approaching when they would be forced from the sands. Every day, great sail less ships chugged along, removing their shoreline. With each tide they were trapped, in a trance like sleep, under the water. Most times they were returned with the next tide, the exception `the great tide`. There was no way of knowing how long this could take you for; it was the one that had taken them for almost two centuries. This was the one that was almost upon them. The only other option was to join the land children. He shivered at the thought. No! He would commit himself and his children to the water first. He thought long and hard on this matter. The land children eyed his band, constantly waiting to capture a straying child, they had become the very essence of evil. The responsibility of it all weighed heavy on him. After a long day and night he came to his decision. He would gather his children, they would enter the water together and maybe when they returned, they too would find a way to be free. He felt calmness, he was weary of this existence, he yearned for eternal rest below the water.

That night he almost filled the sands with his little lost souls. They huddled together, holding hands. Jonathan kept tight hold of Emma, together they prayed out loud as the swelling water approached. The land children rushed to see, they screamed obscenities at Jonathan. He shivered as he prayed, 'Please let them be gone to a place of rest before we return!'

Jonathan's long sleep was interrupted by explosions dropped into the river. The water was blown up and out, exposing the sands. Some of the children escaped for a brief moment, before being sucked back under. What they glimpsed on the shore shocked them. There were many changes. The docks were packed with great iron cargo and war ships. Some children were able to clamber aboard and were trapped when the water crashed back. Others only escaped for brief spells. Overjoyed to be free of their watery grave, they howled when they were sucked back under. Sailors on the late night watch, shivered at the sound. 'Banshee's' they whispered. The children on board found themselves a place to hide. They could see the shoreline, it was greatly changed. Massive stone warehouses, thousands of dock and warehouse workers. They were housed in the four and five story buildings that lined the docks. The ships they were on were war ships, they sat and listened with the sailors. They were shocked to hear they had just come to the end of the second of two world wars.

It would seem the port was prospering. Some of the children stole ashore; they waited on the sands for Jonathan. They felt sure he would return soon, he had been gone for over a century. They only ventured ashore when the tide came. They would huddle together, wary of the land children, who they caught glimpses of in the buildings they called tenements. The children waited for four more decades, they saw with dismay, the port go into decline again. The warehouses were closing down. They sat with the workers in their tea huts as they talked of `a world recession`. There was no work for them, and once again, poverty hit the work force. They watched many of the people move out of the tenements. They were forced to move to the outskirts of the city to find work. The dockland became a barren wasteland again. The great cargo ships moved to the southern ports. The dredges that that had kept the seabed clear were no longer needed, the sands were once again building up.

JONATHAN RETURNS TO BEDLAM

Jonathan opened his eyes; he was lying on his back on the wet sand. Although saddened that he was still earthbound, he was curious as to how long they had been in the water. He struggled to his feet and looked along the sands for his sister. He sighed with relief when he saw her, playing amongst the gulls. It was as if she had never been away. For the first time, he wondered if she had returned with him. He had always assumed that they left and returned together. He looked toward the mouth of the river and was shocked at the changes. Massive warehouses, huge buildings with stone birds on top and giant clocks. He pondered on the year, the century! He knew a vast amount of time had passed, except for the river, it could have been another world. It was early morning, the sun was shining weakly through grey skies, and he guessed it was spring. He looked further ashore where he could see dozens of the spirit children who had returned with him. They were running wild in the warehouses and empty dock sheds, delighted to be free of the water. He felt happy for them. As for himself, he had mixed feelings. He accepted, if nothing else, his passage of time below the waves had helped to resign him to the fact they would never be released. He looked toward the shoreline, to the rows of tenements that lined the waterfront. He had a hundred questions, all these changes. But one loomed above all `the land children`! He shivered at the memory of them, the changes to their bodies. The older ones had taking to loping along on all fours! From a distance, they looked like a pack of dogs. Even the toddlers became like the stray cats, hairy, their little eyes slanted, their little milk teeth now yellow and sharp. The babies, who were only crawling when their souls were stolen, were sprouting small feathers. When they crawled on the sands they looked like the gulls. He decided there and then to stay on the sands until he knew what was ahead for him ashore

The days drifted into weeks and months. He strayed, mostly through loneliness and curiosity, further on to the land. Then urged on by his children, who told him of strange happenings concerning the land children, he approached the tenements. Almost at once, he chanced upon the skeletal brothers. They were greatly changed. He almost had to turn away from their grotesque bodies. Thick, black hair covered their long, bony bodies. Their nails long and thick like yellow talons. There long eyes, blood red. They were stalking a small, lone boy who looked to be about eight. He was wandering toward the riverside, in his hand he held a make shift fishing line. He was totally unaware of the brothers. They were on all fours circling him, urging him on. The boy sat swinging his legs on the dock wall. He dangled his home made net into the water. Jonathan overcame his disgust and fear and ran toward them. He knew what they were about to do, he roared, 'Leave him!' Their heads shot around, their eyes glinted! They looked at each other, and in a swift, rehearsed attack, the younger one reared up. Teeth bared, he attacked Jonathan. As Jonathan fought to be free, he saw the other brother push the boy into the water. He screamed as he saw the brother follow. He could not believe the strength of the snarling half human, who was on his back, biting into his neck. He felt no pain but it was draining his strength. He dragged him along to the waterside. Suddenly, the boy was pushed ashore by the older brother. He kept a tight grip on the boy and snarled at Jonathan. It was plain the boy had drowned. Now in spirit, he whimpered in terror at the sight of his killer.

Jonathan freed himself from the brother; he sprang toward the boy and managed to pull him away.

Suddenly, in front of the boy, a stout, fierce looking spirit woman pointed to Jonathan. 'YOU! BOY!' She ordered. She stood, hands on hips, a furious expression on her round face. 'Send him across, this instant!' The brothers knew she had more power, but they still snarled at her and attempted to approach the boy. She took a step toward them.

The boy, who had been frozen with fear, now came to life. He recognised her 'Nan!' He screamed. He ran toward her, she lifted him without effort.

Jonathan urged the woman to be gone. She turned, and before the howling brothers could do anything, she had disappeared. They looked at the lifeless body floating on the waves. They squealed at him in anger, glaring with devilish burning eyes before scurrying away.

This was the definite parting of the ways for Jonathan. They were totally lost to him; from now on he would keep his distance. Still he watched out for them, especially when he saw them with a newly arrived child, this he could not ignore. When he challenged them, they would say they had found the child wandering `already departed`. They said he or she had been murdered or abandoned; no one had come to claim them. He took no chances and would take the child, ignoring their threats of reprisals. He dreaded that there must be more that they kept hidden from him, until they were lost, doomed to become like them.

There had been another development in the tenements. Voices of the living had started calling to them. He knew not how at first, but then found to his amusement, it was a contraption they called the Ouji board. He followed the voice asking. 'Is anybody there?' He entered their strange homes, but was pushed aside by older, cruel and twisted spirits. They had lived wicked and murderous lives. They could not, or would not, pass over. They used the board skilfully, pretending to be members of their family that had passed over. Once they convinced their victim, they would warn them of family betrayals and looming death. What had started as harmless fun for the players, had filled their homes with evil. Some older spirits had the power of possession, especially if the player was young and susceptible. They picked their host, and when the player left to go home, they were already doomed

They were never to know peace again. Their sleep disturbed, their families haunted. Their homes, under a cloud of depression, never looked the same. The women complained that whatever they did, their home looked dark and shadowy. Jonathan quickly distanced himself, he wanted no part of it. He was unhappy that despite his warning, some of his children were attracted to the séances. They watched with great interest. Soon they began joining in when the older ones got restless and left. Until they too were chased by the dreaded brother's children; they learned quickly how to answer the questions. This made their next step easy; they attached themselves to the weak of minds. Once they controlled a player, they would go home with them. They practised possession. On awakening, the possessed would catch a glimpse of a gruesome child grinning into their face. It turned their minds, leaving them frozen with fear. Once in their house they took over, scurrying around, causing terror in the hearts of the occupants. Their pets sensed them. Some, especially the cats, could see them, they would stand on stiff legs, their backs arched their fur standing on end. They would escape into the night, screeching in the darkness. People trembled in their beds in apprehension. Once they would talk to each other of their little guests, now they sensed evil in the air.

Some land children, who had been earth bound for many centuries, had mastered the power to cross over, be it only for a short time, it would petrify the observer. They chose the weak of mind, the young and the adolescents.

James was one such youth. He had only attended a séance once, it had frightened the life out of him and he had left before the finish, it was too late! As he hurried to his fourth floor flat, the skeletal brothers clung to him. They tormented him until he was a shadow of himself. Every night he sat at the end of his bed, his arms hanging limply at his sides, staring at the floor, afraid to close his eyes. When he finally succumbed to sleep, they would pounce! Whispering right into his ear! Breathing into his face! They lay either side of him. Although awake, he was paralysed with fear! He mumbled prayers, they jumped up and down, laughing! His family lay listening to the frightening sounds, they could sense the evil. What could they do?

Their son was dying in front of them! He would not say what was happening, he never spoke at all, he was gaunt and withdrawn.

It had come to the attention of Jonathan, his children told of the haunting of James. Everyone was waiting for the final act! The taking of his soul! He nodded, he had been expecting something like this, and now, his fears were confirmed. The brothers were so much stronger now. They had never had the power to possess a youth. He could no longer stand back! That night, he watched with despair through the bedroom window. He saw the boy stand facing the wall, his eyes tight shut, his hands covering his ears. Nothing could stop them, they showed no mercy! They screamed at him to jump out of the window. When he did not respond, they pushed him up the wall until his feet dangled above the floor. Jonathan could do nothing! He had none of these powers, he could only appeal to them to spare the boy. They saw him and laughed as he came into the room; he dropped to his knees and begged them to spare James. Suddenly the boy turned, his white face calm, he had decided. They all saw his intent; the brothers opened the doors for him as he walked stiffly to the landing. Jonathan was desperate, what could he do? He could not cross over!

James felt a calmness for the first time since the hauntings had begun. He could take no more! It was the middle of the night, the tenements were deserted and in darkness. He stood and looked over the landing to the square below. He showed no emotion at the terrible sight that greeted him, hundreds of tide children looked up at him. They called to him in their high, squealing voices to 'jump!' Laughing and cheering, the brothers who stood either side of him, gripping his shoulders. The older spirits had joined them. They pushed the squealing children to one side, they too wanted his soul. The brothers hissed in James ear. 'Come James, 'tis time, now it is over!'

Jonathan shouted to the boy. 'NO!' It was to no avail, he could not hear. Slowly, James pulled himself onto the landing wall; he stood with his hands at his side. The children were hysterical! The noise was deafening. Jonathan was distraught; he knew there would be no peace for the boy in death. He looked down at the baying ghouls then blinked with shock! There in the middle, surrounded by a yellow light, stood a lone man. He wore the army uniform of the world war, his face was solemn as he looked up, stiff backed. Jonathan knew instinctively he was the boy's grandfather. He felt his pain; he had no chance against the hordes of evil spirits! Only his brave heart kept him there. James stood, a silence descended for one fleeting second, then he dropped! Without knowing why, Jonathan leapt up behind him, he gripped onto him! It was over in an instant! They hit the ground, the boy's spirit burst from his broken body. In a flash, acting on instinct, Jonathan half ran, half flew toward the soldier with James. The man enveloped him in his arms, and in a blinding flash, they were gone.

The evil spirits went crazy. They tore at him, dragging him the floor. He stumbled toward the river as they rained blows down on him. He felt his spirit weaken, only the memory of the boy in his grandfather's arms kept him going. As they neared the water, some released him, finally they let go. They screamed as he stumbled onto the sand. He lay on his back, trembling; his children crept to him, fearfully looking around. They had seen the monumental battle. It took days for his strength to return, only then did he allow himself to remember, he hardly dared think it was true. For a fleeting moment had his spirit entered the falling boys? This helped him through his convalescence. He reflected on the massive changes, not least to the land children, they were so powerful! The brothers un-recognisable! For the first, time he admitted his feelings of guilt. He should not have left! He should never have entered the great tide. He vowed to himself that from now on, he would concentrate on the souls that could be re-united. Those that had been trapped like him, would be given his protection from the evil ones.

.   The land children were incensed at the loss of the youth. They increased their hauntings, targeting babies, toddlers, infants! They showed no mercy to their easy targets. The infants could see them; they pointed and called to them. The parents laughed nervously at their child's` imaginary friend`. As their baby waved, pointing and whispering in dark corners.

There seemed to be an epidemic of cruelty to the local animals. The streets where strewn with dead dogs, cats and birds. Not just dead, but horribly mutilated! The parents were appalled as they watched it unfold; it had to be the tenants own children, they were out of control.

They were cruel and vicious to anyone weaker than themselves. 'It was like!' They thought silently. 'They were possessed!'

Jonathan watched from a distance, he was at a loss as to what he could do; the possessions were on a massive scale. His children had begun to stray again. They were bored of the sands; Emma begged to go with them. He made her promise not to stray from the others, he understood. He could only hope they would take heed of his warnings. They had been here so long they knew no one would come for them now.

The brothers had more and more followers. Jonathan took it upon himself to patrol the streets and waterfront. He worked relentlessly, thwarting the evil ones attempts to entice local toddlers to their death. For a while it seemed to quieten down. Then it all changed again. Whilst out looking for Emma, he witnessed a terrible sight. The brothers pushed an elderly woman under the wheels of an oncoming car. He was too far away to rescue her spirit, but this time there was no need, her departed husband and family quickly surrounded her and took her to her rest. The children skulked away, they saw Jonathan and scowled at him. He stared back. His strength was back, he would keep good his promise, he would never desert the waterfront again! `They` hated him and swore that one day, somehow, they would destroy him. For now they switched back to the tenements, they knew he was reluctant to enter. They turned their attention back to possession, once again, the adolescents their targets.

Fourteen year old Maria lay on her bed, peeping over the cover. The room was in darkness but she had been born with second sight, she knew she had company. She watched the shadowy children creep toward her bed. She sensed their evil intent, these were not her departed family, they were devils. She sprang to her feet and threw holy water at them, reciting the Latin prayer to Michael the Angel, for the protection from evil. At once they departed; her sleeping family heard and signed themselves with the cross. They thanked God for her gift; they cared nothing for those that said she was `simple`, Worse! Cursed!

Those children without protection were possessed nightly. When they did the terrible things the brothers told them to do, they had no reason to give their broken hearted parents other than. 'I don't know why, only that I had to! Something told me to do it!' To the skeletal brothers delight, no one believed. The half empty tenements were named locally as the `devils playground!`. A crime wave emanated from there, robberies, muggings, even murder!

THE NIGHT OF THE DEMONS

It was a bitterly cold November night, black ice on the ground, the air heavy with a thick, yellow smog. There were hundreds of earthbound spirits abroad, more than usual. Reluctantly, Jonathan took his children further in land, a high tide was expected. The children quickly dispersed, with his warnings of the land children ringing in their ears. They made their way to the homes in the tenements where they had family links from centuries earlier. They would sit amongst them, safe from the evil ones, who for some unknown reason, seemed unable to enter certain homes.

Jonathan was afraid as strange spirits came out of the smog, he saw weird and awful shapes, they were not all human. He had never seen the likes before, nor did he ever want to see again. He took refuge in the shadows in an alley at the back of the local row of shops. His intent was to search for Emma, he now regretted letting her go with the others. He was overtaken by a dread; these older spirits were known to take tide children captive. They were much more powerful than him. It was then he saw a truly chilling and fearsome sight. First, he became aware of someone beside him. It was a living man, he looked to be in his thirties; he was short in stature with oriental features. His black hair was greased and combed straight back, making his profile stand out. In his hand he held a long, white, bone handled, serrated knife. In his heart, murder! He started to speak feverously, seemingly to himself, in a strange tongue. Suddenly, to Jonathan's horror, the man leaned against a devilish spirit. He was as yellow as brine, his coal black eyes were sunk deep in a decomposed face. His twisted mouth drooled a foul smelling liquid. He was communicating with the possessed man in a low, rasping voice.

'The deed must be done this night.' He placed a long, wrinkled, yellow hand on the handle of the knife.

Jonathan trembled violently. The grotesque shape stepped inside the man as if he was donning a cloak. 'Possession' he whispered. He was witnessing it close up for the first time. He froze as the evil ones voice came from the man's mouth.

'Three girls approach, do not let them leave, Diablo wants them, you must release their spirits.' The smell of sulphur coming from his mouth was overpowering. The man's long eyes rolled back in his head, yet they remained black. It seemed he was of no consequence to this powerful demon, he cared not that he was witness. Jonathan remained rooted to the ground. He watched in paralysed silence as the man licked his lips with a thick, black, hairy tongue. 'It is done.' He muttered. 'I will cut their hearts out.'

To Jonathan's stark horror, three young girls in their early teens turned into the alley. Despite their mother's worries that they should stay indoors on a night such as this, they headed for their local youth club, taking this deadly `short cut`. They linked arms, talking loudly of the night ahead. His fear for himself evaporated, he had to stop them! They were seconds away from being massacred by the possessed man, worse! Their souls taken for eternity! He sprung forward, running toward them, not sure what he could do! He started screaming. 'GO BACK! GO BACK!' His big blue eyes were wide with terror, then hopelessness; it was futile! He could not stop what was about to happen, they could neither see nor hear him. He sobbed as they neared the crazed man. The evil entity laughed at his efforts and swore to take him captive when the deed was done.

Suddenly, the elder of the girls, Kate, stopped dead! Her friends stared at her, puzzled; He could hardly dare to hope! Had she sensed something? He stood before her; he could see fear in her eyes as she looked around. He waved his arms in front of her face. Would it be enough?

She shivered and whispered 'someone walked over my grave', she looked down the entry and half turned. 'I don't want to go down there!' A feeling of dread was flooding through her.

Her friends giggled nervously. 'Oh come on!' Her friend Mary urged. 'We don't want to be late.' Against Kate's better judgement, they once again linked arms and hurried ahead. Her friends were now silently regretting their decision to go ahead in this long, narrow, unlit alley. What if they were attacked? Who would hear? They could see nothing ahead, just the outlines of dumped rubbish and dark shadows. They were getting ever closer to the evil one. He howled with wicked glee at Jonathan's useless shouts of warning. Suddenly, out of nowhere, there was a loud cracking sound from above. Then the almighty sound of a sharp wind, it zipped overhead like a jet stream. Everyone looked up, open mouthed! The air stilled, almost to the point of paralysing the girls. No one moved! For the first time, Jonathan witnessed something he had only heard of many times! Above their heads, appeared what he had heard the living describe as `Guardian Angels!` Not the way they imagined them, or they were painted in their churches, as heavenly bodies. These were kin to the girls from generations past. Three middle aged woman, dressed in the fashion of their day. Long dark coats that reached their booted feet, their long platted hair, pinned up on their heads. They were hardly visible as they zipped across at tremendous speeds. He could not see their features. The girls remained still, looking up; they could only hear the noise of the whistling wind. Jonathan sensed something powerful was about to happen. The girls came back to life. They never spoke, they could not! They covered their ears, shielding them from the noise; they stumbled quickly on their deadly way to the exit. They were totally unaware of the crazed man standing in the shadows.

The evil one urged him out; he knew he only had seconds before his power was taken from him. The man raised the knife. The noise suddenly stopped, leaving an electric silence, the air about them changed. Everything appeared as if in black and white, unreal, but it was happening. Both Jonathan and the crazed man stood rooted, looking up, unable to move, as again and again the women made their rescue flights across the paths of the girls. Faster and faster, until for one amazing second, two dimensions became one, for a split second they became visible to the girls.

The petrified girls stood looking up as the woman appeared, flying in slow motion, they held hands, forming a circle above them. Their faces were blurred, but for their clothes, they were neither man nor woman. Time stood still! Then it was over! They could no longer see them, it had happened so quickly it had taken their breath away. Then they screamed in abject terror, they turned and ran and ran faster than ever before, leaving behind the man with his knife still raised.

The evil one recovered his senses and screamed horrible profanities at the women, but he knew it was over. With their combined power, he had no chance. If he had fought them, they could have taken away his strength for centuries to come. He vacated the man violently. He collapsed to the floor, convulsing in dire shock. The demon disappeared into the smog, howling his rage into the night, sounding to the living, like a wolf. They shivered in their homes, wondering what kind of animal made such a haunting sound.

Left on his own to recover, the mentally ill man looked at the knife in his trembling hand. His face was grey, he remembered what he had been about to do? He staggered out; he had to make sure this would never happen again. He looked to the river; he had to end it all.

Jonathan shook too, but not with fear, he was elated. The girls had escaped, but even more! Guardians did exist! He gave a prayer of thanksgiving that he had been privileged to have witnessed it. He secretly hoped for more, did he have a hand in bringing them? He prayed this meant there was still a chance for him. So much had been revealed to him this strangest of nights. Surely he was not doomed to roam this earth for eternity? If others could aspire to be Guardians, was there a chance for him?

The girls ran, without speaking, to their homes, Kate's mother held her sobbing daughter until she could speak. She remained looking calm, inwardly, her heart pounded as the story unfolded. She never doubted it for one instant. 'Guardian angels!' She whispered. Later, as she left her sleeping daughters room, she took out the old family album. She slowly opened it, tears slipped down her cheeks as she looked at the old black and white photograph of her Irish grandmother. She was just as Kate had described her. 'Thank you nan.' She sobbed; she was convinced something terrible had been in store for the girls. Far off memories of her grandmother came flooding back. An immigrant from Ireland, she was a staunch catholic; she was renowned for her gift `second sight!` Although desperately poor herself, she tended to everyone's need before herself. She was known as a living saint. They had lived on the site of the tenements in small houses. It was well known, that although in seemingly good health, her grandmother knew that her time was almost at an end. She had no fear; such was her faith. That was until she saw `them!` They had suddenly appeared, sitting on her back yard wall, staring into her face as she lay in bed.

Kate's mother Irene was just a child of six, her grandmother asked for her to be brought to her bed. When the others left, her Grandmother took her hand, she asked her what she could see on the wall outside; she shrugged her little shoulders 'just the little women with long hair.'

Her grandmother signed herself with the cross. 'Banshees!' She whispered. She had always known the child had her gift. 'They have come for me!' Irene became afraid and called her mother.   No-one could convince the old lady, all they saw were large feral cats. She became agitated. She said was weary, it was time for her to go, but not while `they` where there. 'Be gone!' She shouted. Her family sent for the old Irish parish priest. He listened patiently, his face grave. He looked out of the window then he turned to her and nodded. She sighed with relief, they both said the prayers for the last rites, then he turned to the window, he chanted an incantation in Latin. They both heard the soft crying outside. The old lady took his hand. 'They have gone.' She said softly. She looked up at her white faced family. 'It is my time, God willing, I will look over you!' Irene kissed the photograph 'thank you nan.'

Jonathan slipped out the alley, back into the ghost filled night, his head full of what he had seen. He needed to be back on the sands where he would be safe, but the water was still high. He looked around for Emma, he saw less and less of her lately. He guessed she would be in the tenements; she spent more and more time there, attached to a small sickly girl, the youngest of a large family. He worried that when the child succumbed, as she would, for she had a heart no bigger than a new born, Emma would try to keep her earthbound. He could see the tenements; they made an eerie sight in the smog. Over half of the flats where vacant, those residents who were left, lived in hellish conditions. He feared that the riverside area was going through yet another transition. The families were scattering, the area decimated. Many of his children followed them, having, like Emma, become attached to a family. He was overcome by the eternity of it all. His head hung and he became morose. Why could he not be like the guardians? He was in awe of their great power. How did you get this? What or who gave it to you? He suddenly became chillingly aware of a presence. He turned slowly, hardly daring to look. A spirit man stood looking at him through the thick smog. Jonathan could sense no threat from him, he relaxed a little. He dressed in a dark suit of the present day. His stature, tall and slim. His collar length hair as black as coal. His thick eye lashes framed the bluest of eyes, set in a refined pallid face. He was, Jonathan thought, `ageless!` He sensed he had come to him for a reason. He waited, struck dumb. He knew he was in the presence of a higher, more powerful spirit.

The man smiled down gently at the boy. 'Your time on earth is well spent.' His voice filled the night. Strong, yet quiet. 'You have become known as Jonathan, the guardian of lost souls.'

Jonathan could only stand, open mouthed.

The man spoke again. 'Your time will come, you have earned the right. Your mother will come for you.'

Jonathan was overwhelmed, his eyes welled with tears. He had! He had come to visit him! The first since his mother. Was he his Guardian Angel? Was it finally at an end?.

The man turned into the night. Jonathans eyes filled with disappointed tears, he had not told how long. He found his voice. 'Master!' He called. The man turned, 'When?' He asked weakly, afraid of the answer, yet desperately needing to know.

The man smiled. 'What is time to you? Only to know you will free is enough.' His face became serious. 'Now tend to your work. The evil one is strong, remember he is in fire and water' He looked to the tenements. 'There is much activity there. Even as I speak, a family is in danger. Two brothers have joined forces with the evil one!'

Before he could ask more, he was gone! He shook with excitement as he went over the message and the warning; it had to be the skeletal brothers! He had not come across them for a long time. They never came to the sands, afraid of the water, scared they would be trapped by the tide. He had tried not to think of them, they filled him with feelings he did not like, he deeply abhorred them. They were the instigators of his trapped existence. Now he must face his demons! He hurried to the tenements, almost at once he could hear them. They were in a ground floor flat where a large family lived. They had attached themselves to two of the young daughters. The father of this brood was a dour, bull of a man. He drank far too much and terrorised his family. The alcohol made it easy for the brothers to turn his mind; they pushed and shoved him around the house. He would roar with terror at the sisters, blaming them, saying it was only when they were around he suffered so. Indirectly he was right! The brothers got an evil enjoyment watching the sisters suffer at the hands of their demented father.

Jonathan watched through the window. His heart went out the family as the father drove them to hide in terror in their bedrooms. Now the man was trying to light a cigarette, shouting and cursing at the air around him, raging at his invisible tormentors. He put the cigarette in his mouth. Swaying, he took a large piece of newspaper, he put it into the blazing coal fire, it burst into flames! Jonathan was horrified at the look of pure evil that passed between the brothers. He knew they were going to do something! What new powers had they been given by their master?

The drunken man put the flaming paper to his lips; the younger boy snatched the cigarette from his mouth. The man looked around, startled! 'Who did that?' He whispered.

The cigarette flew across the room, then back again. The boys laughed hysterically. Jonathan feared they were not on their own. They had never crossed over with such power before. He stole a look around; there was no one, except for an old, grey, feral cat. It watched with green, slanted eyes through the now smoky window. Its back arched with pleasure, Jonathan knew the evil one possessed it. The boys were greatly excited by their new power. They blew at the flames, causing ash and burning paper to scatter around the room. The terrified man threw it into the fire, his bloodshot eyes bulging with fright. The younger boy caught it and carried toward his face. The man fell backwards over the armchair. All he could see was the burning paper being carried toward him by invisible hands. The boys were becoming more demonic! Dancing around him, pinching and pulling. Suddenly the man caught a glimpse of them, their long, thin, hairy faces; sunken eyes; long, black, broken teeth; rags hanging off their dog like bodies! They were a horrific sight. Even in his drunken state; he knew they were children of the devil! He fled, screaming like a lunatic out of the house, leaving the burning paper on the fireside rug. The rush of air dramatically fed the flames. Jonathan could hide no longer, the rug was ablaze. Putting his own safety aside, he rushed into the room. The boys jumped back, they screeched at him, startled by his appearance. Before Jonathan could tackle the fire, the grey cat manifested itself in the flames! Jonathan fell back; he had never seen anything as hideous as this form. He thought it had to be the evil one himself, if not, certainly his close companion! He knew for sure that such was the pure terror it instilled to any live victim who saw it, they would surely die! A stench of sulphur and brine filled the air. It stood amongst the flames, barring his way. Its long fingers armed with thick, black talons. Its hooved feet almost unnoticeable when you saw its head, huge, shaped like a goats, complete with horns! Its eyes, that of a serpent! Jonathan was rooted to the floor, he could not move. The fire was becoming an inferno. The brothers ran around like little, hairy devils! They were gloating at Jonathan's helplessness against the creature before him. The flames had spread out of the room; acrid, black smoke billowed from the flock filling in the old furniture. It's suffocating fumes filling the flat, spreading to the bedrooms!

There was no time to waste. With great energy, he knew not from where, he closed his eyes and roared. 'WAKE UP! WAKE UP! FIRE! FIRE! Instantly he found himself at the bedside of the mother, she was almost overwhelmed, half conscious. Her eyes shot open! In an instant she was out of the bed! She screamed to her family, they heard, they too shouted their warnings to the rest of the family.

Jonathan stood trembling, he had done it! He had crossed over! Be it only for a moment and just in time! The family fell out into the freezing night, holding each other, in shock. They looked around. Where was the boy? He had surely saved their lives with his frantic calls of fire! The flat was burned to a shell. The neighbours huddled around in shivering groups. None doubted the mother's story of the boy who woke her. The older ones nodded seriously. 'A guardian angel!' they said. The others shivered, they signed themselves with the cross, comforting the crying family.

Jonathans work with the family was done. He shuddered, he was not going back into that flat. The brothers were lost to him, he knew he could never save them. He determined to keep watch over the tenements, the strangers warning rang in his ears, it was true, the evil one was abroad in them! He had to get Emma away from these cursed homes, persuade her to leave them. As he turned, he felt eyes burning through him! He caught a flash of the brothers. They were still in the shell of the flat, scowling, waiting for the next family. He could delay no longer, he hurried to where he knew his sister would be. He found her in a dimly lit bedroom; Emma lay alongside the sick girl. She frowned when she saw him, refusing his pleas to leave the child Jane who was talking to her. The child could see her clearly; he knew this was because she was almost crossed over. He could see his sister adored her, kissing her frail face, playing games, she sang to her. Once the child sang along too, in a hauntingly thin, high voice. He froze as he listened.

We are children of the tide, under the water we do hide

Calling, calling!

He stared at Emma accusingly; it was the brother's song!. She glared back, unrepentant. She cared not that he knew her intention. She was determined to keep Jane.

'GO AWAY!' She spat vehemently, baring her teeth. Jonathan gasped, they were long and pointed.

The little girl saw him, she repeated what Emma had said, 'go away!' Although weak, her voice carried.

Her family rushed into the room. Her frightened mother whispered. 'What is it Jane?'

The child sobbed, 'He won't go! He is going to take my Emma!'

Her parents looked fearfully around the small room, her mother's voice trembled. 'Who is Emma? Who is going to take her? Who is Emma?'

Jane's face had turned a ghastly blue, her black eyes big and wild, her nostrils pinched, her small rib cage rose rapidly up and down. Her mother caught her breath; she reached for her child's hand. 'Stay with us baby.' She pleaded futilely, knowing she was near her end.

Emma pulled at her hand, her little thin face twisted. 'NO! You come with me! You promised! We're going on the sands, we will play in the water! You promised!'

The girl cried out to her mother. 'Let me go! I need to go, please mammy!' The excitement was too much! Her little heart fluttered and failed.

Emma was as quick as lightning, as the child's spirit left her body she leapt toward her. Almost instantly another shape stood at the awakening girl's side. An elderly, white haired man. He saw Emma and bravely barred her way. Emma stood back agape. To Jonathan's horror, she attacked him with all the fury of a lioness. It took the man by surprise, he fell backwards. Jonathan was frozen, this was not sweet Emma, she was possessed! She screamed at the bewildered child. 'Run! He is a bad man!'

The child fled from the house, past her sobbing parents and distraught siblings, all unaware of the fight for their little ones spirit. Jonathan sprang back to life, he chased after Jane, but it was too late. She was already in the square, surrounded by dozens of excited, evil land children. Now she was scared! She cried out for her mammy.

Jonathan called to her franticly. 'Do not go! Come back! The man is your grandfather!' He felt teeth sink into his almost transparent neck. He hardly felt the pain, but he could not loosen the grip. He knew without looking, it was Emma. Like a demon from hell she clung. He was distraught! His baby sister was she completely lost to him. 'No!!' He raged. 'I must get her back! I must!' Somehow he knew. that when his mother returned, he must have Emma with him. She would not rest without her. She would think he had neglected his duty. Instead of fighting to get her off, he held her small, claw like hands.

She realised what he was about to do, she struggled desperately to be free. She screamed to the brothers children for help. 'He is taking me to the water!'

  They attacked him in numbers. He hardly recognised them as the lost frightened souls that first joined his group. Their eyes; blood red slanted, they attached themselves to him with their teeth and claws. He fought to struggle to the docks, he had to reach the water or she would be lost to him forever. This way she could be gone for a day or decades, there was no way of knowing. For a while at least, he would know she was safe. He failed to see or hear the child Jane running desperately behind them. She had broken free during the battle, she was sobbing with fright. He threw his screaming sister into the deep swell. To his horror, Jane swiftly followed! He stood, his head in his hands; there was nothing he could do. He would have to keep vigil, wait for the returning tide; hopefully she would return to her Grandfather. He was standing next to Jonathan, wringing his hands in despair. Jonathan tried to comfort him, he was inconsolable.

He shook his head. 'I have failed her! She is doomed to become a lost soul! I too will be earthbound, I cannot leave without her.'

No amount of comfort could assure him that she would return. He left Jonathan, his white head low, heading back to the tenements.

The dawn was breaking, the water gently subsided. Jonathan waited on the dockside, praying for their return. The waves broke upon the sand, the children of the tided emerged. Some crawling, as if from a long sleep. Others running, embracing their freedom from the murky salty water. He searched amongst them. He heaved a huge sigh of relief, amongst the crowd he saw Emma had come back! He did not know who decided the length of time you rested in the water, he was just grateful. She looked like her old self, skipping along the sand. She saw him and smiled as she called to him. He was overcome with relief, he thanked God, at her side was Jane! She looked happy, content. They held hands as they ran towards him. He embraced them warmly. The morning mist was dispersing, he looked for the grandfather. He silently worried that if he didn't re-unite them quickly, Emma would become attached again.

Jane followed his gaze and saw the tenements. She cried out with delight. 'Mama! Dada!' They hurried to keep up with her. She called to the neighbours as she passed and frowned when they ignored her. He did not have the heart to tell her they could not see her. As they approached her flat, he saw the white sheets up on the windows. He knew it was to symbolise the family was in mourning. He knew the customs of the residents, there would be a wake before the funeral. The coffin would be open! The child would be terrified to see her own corpse! But she was already at the door! Suddenly, to his relief, the grandfather appeared. He was elated to see her and he held out his arms, she ran to him. Then she heard a sound that halted her, it was her mother sobbing. Before they could stop her, she flew into the room! Her mother sat alone beside the little white coffin.

The child looked in at her dead body, 'Ah' She whispered, her pretty face softened at the sight of her frail, dead body.' She sighed and whispered 'Poor Jane!' She took her mother's hand and kissed her on her cheek with cold lips, She smiled. 'I am going with granddad.' She whispered. 'Where I will be well again, I will wait for you Mama, don't cry.'

The grieving woman seemed to sense her presence; she touched her cheek and smiled softly. 'Oh sweet baby, I can smell you! You are here! Don't you fret, granddad will mind you until I come.' She crooned. She felt a great sense relief. Her child's spirit lived on, she was sure she was here with her. Her chest rose with emotion. 'Look after her, dad!' She prayed aloud. 'I give her to you.'

The child leapt up into her grandfather's arms, eager to be gone. Jonathan looked at Emma, her mouth puckered. 'I want to go!' She cried.

The grandfather did not acknowledge her. He put Jane on his shoulders. Jonathan felt his heart would break at the sobs that tore through Emma. He picked her up. 'One day our mother will come for us.' He promised. He held her tightly until her crying subsided and she quietened. He swore, in future he would keep her close.

EMMA'S REVENGE

Time had gone by, already it was summer. The nights were short, the land children had more and more time for their sinister hauntings. They were encouraged by `the brothers`, their little faces had grown long, their ears pointed, their teeth canine. The tenant's pets were in great fear of them, howling and growling into the dark corners in the homes. Outside, the cats constantly cried, keeping the residents awake. Those that had the gift, shivered, afraid to look out of their windows, knowing the shadowy children who glared back were not of this world!

Jonathan was told by his children of the increase in the gangs of land children. The Skeletal brothers were capturing more and more souls. He felt helpless. All his time was taken protecting his children. He could only watch and pray for the poor souls, who, once captured by them, would never have eternal rest.

The children told him news of the `burnt out flat`, it had been repaired, worse! Re-let! The new tenants were in similar, dire circumstances to the last ones. Four small children, the father `a drunkard`, His harassed wife was at her wits end, her only comfort `the church`, she was a devout Catholic. She prayed for her wayward husband, that he would give up the drink, stop the nightly beatings. No matter how fervently she prayed, as she lay in bed feigning sleep, she would hear him stumbling into the house. Swearing, threatening! The children would huddle together, their hands over their ears, cursing their father to hell. They had company! At their bedside, the brothers slobbered at the prospect of an easy possession.

The man's brain was almost dead. He lay in a drunken stupor in front of the unlit fire. It had been set with paper and coal for the morning, the grinning brother's lit it! The man grew restless with the suffocating heat. Sweat poured down his red, bloated face. They pinched his face, pulled at his hands and feet. One bloodshot eye opened, then another. He cursed loudly. 'Who is it?' He felt claws dig into his shoulders, he was dragged screaming from the chair. He lurched forward! They caught him before he hit the floor. The brothers screeched with delight at their increasing powers. His terrified wife opened the door, he hurtled past her, his face fixed in a silent scream. He hit the wall with great force and fell to the floor, unconscious. The last faces he saw, were two wolf like boys circling him.

Jonathan heard of the family's terrible plight, his children warned of the brothers great powers. All he could do was pray for their victims.

The family watched it unfold in terror, their father faded before their eyes. He screamed at his invisible demons. He howled to Jesus for redemption. His wife watched his possession in horror. The doctors diagnosed `progressed liver disease` too far gone for even his now total abstinence to help. They said this explained his delusions, she was not so sure. She had seen him lifted and thrown across the room! When he pointed and screamed to the corners of his room, she too felt the oppressive atmosphere in the house. The children were awoken nightly by children whispering, scuffling. Neighbours hurried past the flat, they remembered too well what had happened to the previous family. Some that professed to have knowledge of hauntings. were convinced they had `Poltergeists`.

The haunted man was dying! He lay rambling, shouting at his tormenters. In one of his saner moments, he begged his wife to get him out of the house 'Away from them!' She begged his sister to let him spend what time he had left in her house on the outskirts of the city. The family heaved a sigh of relief when she agreed. Without delay, he was moved. The brothers were infuriated; they had been within days of taking his soul. Now they turned their attention to the children. They were relentless, showing no mercy! They smashed their possessions! Dragged their sheets off the bed! The mother could take no more! She turned to the church for help. The parish priest listened. Although sympathetic, he knew the history of the family. Inwardly he agreed with the doctors, but he knew the family needed more. He gave her a bottle of holy water and promised he would pray for peace in her home.

She sat trembling, waiting for the children to go to their beds. She placed the holy water on the table, surrounded by her holy statues. She picked up her black rosary beads and put them around her neck. A noise at the window made her jump with fright. She sighed with relief, it was just a stray, grey cat that had taken to sitting on her window ledge. The brothers stood silent, watching her, she reached for the bottle. They looked at each other and sprang into action. She saw nothing as she was swung around the room by the rosary beads. They snapped and scattered, the bottle of water was smashed against the wall. She stood rooted, her eyes wild with fear, a scream trapped in her throat. The brothers were incensed, they howled as they took her holy pictures and statues and threw them at her. She fell to the floor, curled in a ball! They turned their attention to the children; they went into the bedrooms and dragged the screaming children from their beds. The mother half crawled, half fell, into the room. They clung to each other as they ran out into the night, taking only what they could carry. They never returned!

The neighbours hurried past the vacant flat in the following weeks. They swore there was more noise emanating from the vacant flat than before. In small groups, they whispered of ghostly sighting of small, ragged children seen at the windows.

Jonathan listened to it all in despair. What could he do on his own? He had to look over his children. They still frequented the families that held no threat to them. Emma begged to be allowed to sit in Jane's flat. She said she felt comforted by the family. Reluctantly he agreed. He had neglected his duties as guardian of the tenements, this would allow him some freedom. He told her sternly that he would keep watch on her. She, in turn, promised she would not become attached again to a living child. He remembered with a shiver, how she had started to master `possession`. If this had progressed, she would have been lost to him forever.

Emma's eyes narrowed with burning hatred when he left. She was glad to be rid of him, his constant talking of a mother she had no memory of. She detested him for spoiling her hauntings with the brothers. She cursed his power to re-unite, even more. It stopped her from doing what she craved, haunting with the brothers! She longed to roam the dockside with them, `they` at least, accepted their eternal fate. No one would ever come for them! It had been centuries....,

She hurried to the tenements and smiled. For now, she would content herself with revenge on Jane's family. She joined them at their fireside, they were reminiscing about

Jane. She hated them. She roamed around the flat. She looked at the large photograph in a glass frame on the wall, `The Grandfather!` She waited; one by one they retired to their beds. She noted how the mother blew a kiss at the photograph. She searched around; she went to the windows looking for her brother. When she was satisfied there were no witness', she took the picture and smashed it, with great force, on the floor! The family burst into the room! They looked around for the source of the noise. The mother pointed to the smashed picture, she cried bitter tears. 'It's ruined!' She sobbed. 'It was the only one. Look! The picture is torn!'

It wasn't enough for Emma, she was restless. Her progress in crossing over was almost complete. She remembered that Jane's aunt lived next door. Her eyes glowed, they had a daughter Mary who was almost ten, but she had the mental age of a three year old. Her and Jane looked alike, her mother used to bring her in to visit her sick cousin. She knew Mary could see her, she too had the gift. Back then, Emma had ignored her. She had been of no interest to her, but now! She licked her lips. 'Perfect!' She whispered. She hovered outside, peering through the window. Mary sat alone in a small, dimly lit living room, in front of a blazing coal fire. She was turning the pages of well fingered picture book. Her mother Myra stood at the sink in the small kitchen, washing clothes. Emma entered the candle lit room, her nose wrinkled, 'what is that smell?' She mumbled. She looked around. The sweet sickly smell seemed to come from the candles. The walls were covered in holy pictures and crucifixes. There was all manner of religious artefacts, some she had never seen before. She looked at them with disdain; they had no effect on the land children. Only the smell disturbed her. She made a note that when she had finished with the girl, she would blow them out. She stood looking down at Mary. The child looked up, she saw her and smiled, Emma sat down beside her.

Mary showed her the book and opened a page. 'Look.' She pointed to a picture of a dog.

Emma glared at her, the child recoiled. She snatched the book and stood up, Marys lip puckered, 'Mine!' She cried. Emma grinned, showing her fangs, the child whimpered. Emma walked to the fire, ready to throw it in the flames. Suddenly, a woman's low, yet menacing voice, filled the room. 'I've been waiting for you! You little devil! Put that down NOW!' Emma jumped back with shock! The book

dropped to the floor. It was Marys' mother, Myra. She was a tall, stocky woman, with striking blue eyes. They held no fear of the grotesque child before her. Instead, she looked furious. In her hands she held a prayer book and a bowl filled with a yellow liquid. She walked fearlessly toward a shrinking Emma. The obnoxious smell was getting stronger. Emma backed away from it, trying to make sense of what was happening. She bared her teeth and spat at the woman. The woman narrowed her eyes. 'You don't scare me!' Her eyes blazed. 'Oh yes! I saw you with Jane! I knew what your game was! You evil daughter of Satan!' She was getting nearer to the spitting, cowering Emma. 'I kept my silence then because you amused Jane!'
Emma felt strange. She tried to extend her talons, ready to attack. Nothing happened! She looked at her hands, they were fading! She was fading! The woman put her fingers into the bowl. Emma could not escape as she threw a foul smelling liquid over her! She knew she was in imminent danger from this powerful woman! Myra opened the book; she called out to Michael and Gabriel! In a high, strong voice, she recited a strange incantation. Emma tried to run past her. The woman threw more of the oil over

her. Emma was desperate to get out! She turned to the window and jumped!

She lay on her back on the sand. Her head would not clear, she tried to make sense of what had just happened. She knew one thing for sure; she had got out just in time. She recalled the stories of homes in the tenements that even the brothers would not enter. She had heard of those living that had the power of exorcism. She had never believed, until now!

It took weeks for her to fully recover. She skulked around, keeping close to the sands. Jonathan was delighted, mistaking her reluctance to stray as a sign she had left the land children for good.

She took this time to keep watch on the tenements. Her hatred for the woman Myra, festering. She knew what she would do if she got the chance. Myra never left the child, she took her everywhere with her. That was until, one early Monday morning, she finally got her opportunity. She saw Myra hurry from the tenements, she was on her own. Her eyes glowed. She rushed to the flat but Mary wasn't there. She backed away quickly from the smell. Out on the landing, she heard the neighbours speak of the child Mary. They said she was sick `some sort of fever`. Her mother had left her with her sister while she went to get the doctor. Emma's eyes flew to Jane's house, she looked through the window. The child was in Jane's old bedroom. Her eyes closed, Emma sniffed at the air, it was clear! Jane's mother fussed around Mary, wiping her forehead, covering her. She looked at the candle her sister had left lit at the bedside. She had blown it out as soon as she had left, afraid it would cause a fire. She accepted her sisters strange practises, people said she had second sight. She herself chose not to believe in the tales of evil that abounded. Content the child was comfortable, she left the room and went outside. She looked over the landing to see if her sister was coming.

Emma was slobbering with excitement, she hovered length ways over Mary's body, their faces touched, the child stirred, Mary opened her eyes, blood red eyes looked back at her! She opened her mouth to scream. Too late! Emma's cold lips covered hers!

Jonathan had been looking for Emma, she had left the sands. He hurried, wanting to find her before the brothers. Of late, she had been so content away from them. He hoped he would find her in Jane's. He made his way there and looked through the window. What he saw broke his heart. Emma lay on top of a small girl. As the child gasped out, Emma inhaled, the girl hyperventilated, Emma sucked in her breath as she exhaled! Jonathan was paralysed! His sister was about to take possession of the child! He had to take great care not to startle Emma, the child could die! He hid, his brain almost bursting! How long had she been able to do this? He watched with horror as Emma entered the child. She stood up, then walked around in a trance like state, her eyes red, unseeing! Obscene words spat out of her mouth. She walked to the third floor window of the bedroom and opened it. Jonathan could wait no longer! He knew what she was about to do! Once she had fallen to her certain death, her soul would be doomed! With as much energy as he could muster, he dived on the girl. At the same time, he roared a warning to her aunt.

'DANGER!' He could only pray she heard.

The girl convulsed and collapsed to the floor! Emma sprang from her! Her face contorted! She screeched in fury! Fighting him with everything she had! Her teeth! Her talons! He was shocked at her strength! She had the power of a demon! Still, he held on! The child Mary crawled along the floor. Her Auntie ran in the room and looked around, white faced, for the boy who had shouted her. She scooped up the limp child. She looked back at the empty room. Shocked, she noted the open window. Her heart pounded even more when Mary looked up at her and whispered huskily. 'Naughty Emma!'

Jonathan jumped! Once again, as in years gone by, he ran the gauntlet of the brother's children. They screamed and howled like wild animals! Enraged he was taking their `future leader!` He never stopped; he knew without the brothers, they would not approach him. They were everywhere. Their hollow eyes glared at him from almost every window.

As they neared the water, his children ran after him. They screamed his name. 'Jonathan! Don't leave us!' He could not stay! He too, was afraid of going into the water. He did not know when, or worse, what, he would return to! He looked at his sister. She was unrecognisable, more animal than child! A foul smelling froth burst from her mouth. He had no choice! He entered the grey murky water! Many of his children followed, not wanting to be left with the demons!

ETERNITY CALLS

They returned at early dawn. As before, they did not know
how long they had been below the water. Jonathan
counted a score or more of his children, He followed them
out, wading out on the sands. He searched along the shore
for Emma; the seagulls saw them and soared high,
screaming down at them. The hair on the back of a stray
dog stood on end, it yelped and tore away. He was used to
the animal's reaction to them. He hurried forward, the
children followed. His head was full of questions. The first
as before, how long had they been away! Had Emma
returned before them? If so, his time in the water had
been wasted! He looked further up the water's edge; he
grew excited at the sight of a little girl running ahead, he
was almost sure it was Emma. Suddenly a spirit woman
appeared before him, she looked elated to see him. She
was middle aged, her long, black hair blew behind her. He
could see by her faded image, she was ready to pass over.
This was a sign she had died at least a generation ago.
She held out her hand to halt him. 'Boy,' she called, in a
frail voice. 'I have been waiting for you. I have come for my
little girl'

He hesitated. He did not want to lose sight of Emma, but he could not refuse. She looked so sad, already she was fading away. He asked her child's name.

'Beth.' She whispered. 'She was five when she drowned.'

He knew at once who she was. He himself had rescued her from the brothers. They had drowned her and taken her spirit. He called to the children 'Tell Beth someone wants her.' The child ran forward. She recognised her mother at once and leapt into her arms. He smiled at their joy as they waved goodbye. It was only then that he looked at the surroundings. There had been massive changes since he was last here. The vacant dock warehouses were once again occupied, people lived in them. Large expensive cars were parked outside, sailing ships were berthed in the docks, He gasped! Tall houses stood where once there were sheds. These were prosperous dwellings, he could hardly believe it. These changes had not happened overnight. They must have been gone at least two decades! He looked up the hill for Emma and gasped! The tenements had gone! In their place were rows of houses, each with their own garden. They did not look as prosperous as the houses on the dock itself, but still a far cry from the tenements. He could see, in the rising sun, spirit children roaming around. Some looked lost and forlorn; others had the animalistic features that came with their dabbling with the evil one. They glared at him, then turned and loped away on all fours! Suddenly, a group of children came running toward him, their faces lit up, delighted to see him. He laughed at their excitement. They were his children who had been left behind. He almost fell to the floor as they clung to him. He settled them down around him on the grass. There was much he needed to know, they had much to tell him. He elected Tom to be their speaker, but first he asked the question. 'What is the year?'

Tom put his hand up, making Jonathan smile. 'It is nineteen ninety.' Jonathan was surprised. He thought he had been away longer than two decades. He pointed up to the houses. 'Start at the beginning, tell me how this all happened.'

The boy leaned forward. 'First they moved out all the tenants, they were scattered all around. Some of our children went with them. Some of us stayed by the water waiting for you' He then answered the question Jonathan was frightened to ask. He leaned forward and lowered his voice. 'The brothers stayed. They moved into the dock estate.'

Jonathan urged him on, Tom continued. 'The area was derelict. For some years there was nothing on the land! Then they started building the new houses, they built houses on the dock itself!' He could hardly contain himself as he continued. 'Then we got a shock! When the tenants finally moved in, we knew them! They were from the tenements!'

Jonathan's eyes opened wide, he didn't understand! 'Why? After all they had endured!'

Tom shrugged, 'They wanted to be together,' Jonathan nodded, he understood. Now he needed to know what happened next, when the brothers children returned. He did not need to ask, Tom grew serious. 'At first, it was just us who moved in with our previous tenants. Many of the older residents got their houses `cleansed`'. Jonathan nodded, feeling some relief. He knew this `ritual`, more importantly, he knew it worked. Tom sighed, 'sadly, many, especially the younger families, just got them blessed! As you remember, it is not enough! Some did nothing at all, they suffered the worse. ' Jonathan hung his head; he knew what was coming next. 'The brothers?' He whispered. They all nodded and moved closer together. Tom shook his head 'not like before. They are stronger, more evil!' He stopped. Just talking about them made him tremble. 'They possessed our homes. The tenants were used to us, we loved being with them, they called us `their guests`. That was until the hauntings began! The brothers have completely possessed two brothers. They have corrupted them.' His voice lowered 'they have even committed murder!'

Jonathan wrung his hands. He felt so guilty for leaving them. They comforted him. He looked at their little faded faces. If ever he had the power, he would give them eternal rest, 'You do understand why I had to go?' He asked brokenly. They all quickly nodded, Tom patted his arm. 'To save Emma!'

He looked around. 'I have to find her!'

Tom pointed to the sands. 'Look, she is playing with the gulls.'

Jonathan was about to stand, Tom shook his head. 'There is more.' They all looked at each other. Jonathan sat. He had to know what he had to face. Tom looked at him sympathetically. 'The girl Mary!' Jonathan nodded. Tom lowered his eyes. 'You must understand! We could do nothing!'

Jonathan frowned. 'Tell me!'

Toms lip quivered. 'We could only watch through the window! They tormented her! Every night they entered her dreams, she had horrific nightmares. They swung her around by her hands, they sucked out her breath until she convulsed!'

Jonathan interrupted. 'But what of her mother? She had the gift! She could have exorcized them!' Tom shook his head. 'She passed, almost two years ago. Jonathan, she was almost eighty. It was her time! She lived alone.'

Jonathan felt terrible guilt. Emma had started this. He grew animated 'Her aunt! Jane's mother! Where is she?' Tom shook his head sadly, 'She lived next door. She watched over her, but she would not let Jane have her candles, for fear of fire! She did not understand!' Tom continued. 'She killed herself Jonathan! They handed her the knife and screamed into her face until she cut her own throat!' Jonathan held his head in his hands. Tom put his arm around him, his face lit up. 'But they never got her soul! Her mother fought them! She took their power for months.'

Jonathan thanked God for that. Tom hung his head. 'They came back! Even more evil and powerful than before! The young men and adolescents suffer the most. They have already driven two of the young men to take their lives! As we speak they are taking possession of a young mother! They enter her nightly as soon as she closes her eyes. When she turns to tell her husband, she finds an empty space!' Tom shivered 'They lay next to her! When she runs down to her husband, he tries to comfort her, he tells her that she is having nightmares! How can he tell her that he hears ghostly boys giggling in their bedroom! Or that when she goes upstairs to bed, he hears footsteps behind her!' Tom looked around, afraid; his voice so low, Jonathan had to struggle to hear. 'They give the older souls to Him! He gives them their power, He is forever at their sides.' Jonathan trembled as he asked. 'Has a grey cat appeared?' They all looked fearfully at Tom as he whispered. 'Do you remember the old lady? She had the gift!' Jonathan nodded. 'Mrs Jones.' Tom said sadly. 'The brothers could not enter her house, she had powerful guardians!' Jonathan remembered her well. Tom's eyes filled with tears. 'He! Came for her! In the form of a grey cat! She allowed him in!' Jonathan was aghast, they all knew to invite the evil one was fatal! 'What about her guardians?'

Tom shook his head. 'They fought all night for her! The poor old lady, she had a night from hell as they battled for her!' He fell quiet as he remembered. He looked at Jonathan and forced himself to continue. 'Her family found her the next morning, her face down on the floor!'

Jonathan shivered. He himself had seen the cat manifest. Tom continued shakily. 'The family believed she had fallen over the stray cat that had been seen on her window sill!'

'Her soul?' Jonathan asked quietly. Tom shook his head. Jonathan felt a terrible fear. He remembered the three guardians he had seen do battle for the three girls. They had seemed so powerful. He hid his fear from them. 'There was once a girl, Kate, she would be a woman now. Did she move back?' Tom nodded. 'How does she fare against them?'

The boy smiled, relieved to be able to give a glimmer of hope to him. 'She is well. She herself is a mother of two, she keeps them well protected. Even before she moved in, she had the house cleansed. She spreads the word. The other tenants think well of her. They told her of their hauntings, especially with their children. They were terrified that they could see whoever made the noises in their homes. They pointed to dark corners, afraid of `the boogie man! ` The toddlers spoke to them in their garbled language. She totally believed them and has convinced a lot of them to get their homes cleansed. The brothers hate her!'

Jonathan stood; he could not let the children see how afraid he was. 'So! My little flock.' He asked lightly. 'Where do you shelter now?' They pointed to a derelict boat docked in the harbour. 'It is safe there, `they' do not come by the water.' He looked at the boat, they were right, it was ideal. 'Then we too will stay there. I must go to my sister. Now, more than ever, I must keep her close!' The children followed him as he looked for her. He prayed to who he hoped was `his` guardian, to give him the strength to take on this battle. He looked around, where had she had gone? He was overcome by a dread! Had she gone to the houses? He searched the sands, calling her name, his shoulders slumped. He wasn't sure he was strong enough yet. He looked at the children, they guessed his intention. Their faces became fearful, he straightened his shoulders, he prayed again for help. He had no other choice. Time was of the essence, he would have to go to the houses. He turned to Tom. 'Go to the boat and wait for me. Just tell me where Jane's mother lives.'

Tom whispered the number. 'Twelve, Jonathan.' He warned. 'It is not protected!'

As he entered the estate, he could feel the evil. Shadowy figures peered at him from almost every corner and house. He tried not to show his fear as he entered the house...

She sat alone in front of the fire. She turned and jumped up. She ran to him, her little face lit up by a big smile. He felt greatly relieved she looked so well, so glad to see him. He thanked God that the time under the water had cleansed her. 'I have so much to tell you brother.' He looked at her, puzzled. She quickly enlightened him, her eyes shining. 'When I was in the water, I saw her! Jonathan, I saw our mother!' He was shocked into silence. It was unheard of to have a memory whilst under the water. Yet she was so convincing, she was glowing as she continued. 'She is so beautiful, she held me. I did not know how much she loved us. She told me we will both be re-united. She has been waiting for you to finish your work. She said you have earned your rest now I must take over, I must atone before I follow!' He tried to take in what she was relating to him, What she said sounded so convincing.

He knelt before her, looking into her face, he had been fooled before! She smiled as he asked. 'Why you Emma? How could you lead the children?'

Her face grew serious. 'Because I have much to pay penance for. I will have to prove to you that I can be trusted before you go.' He was wary. 'How can you do that?'

She sounded so grown up as she answered. 'Because of my knowledge of the brothers and my dabbling's with the evil one! I will have an advantage, they trust me!' He lowered his eyes at her admission. It was so painful for him to hear. She touched his hand. 'I am so sorry my brother, but I have to be completely honest. Mama is going to come for you, we have to start now!' She pleaded

He was in turmoil. This was the last thing he expected. He stood to clear his head. 'When is this happening?'

Emma's face broke into a smile. 'That is what I asked! Mama laughed, I am to say to you 'what is time to you! Just to know is enough!''

He gasped! How could she know that? He looked into her little face, so clear since her rest in the water, and her little- teeth, the fangs where gone. He felt like his heart would break. More than anything he wished he could believe in her, how could he? He took her hand 'No more sister, I am weary, I will not do this anymore!'

Her eyes widened, she looked desperate. 'No! You must not stop now! If need be, I will stay with your children. I will have nothing to do with it. But the residents, they should not pay for my sins!'

Again, she shocked him with her words of wisdom. She took his hand. 'The brothers are gaining. They are causing much heartache! They truly are children of the evil one!' Her eyes glistened with tears. 'You have done so much. Rest! Take time to think of what Mama has said. I will not cause you any more worry.'

He put his head in his hands. How could he say he was scared, more! Terrified! He needed help!

She seemed to know his thoughts. 'I am stronger than I look Jonathan!'

He looked into her eyes. 'That is what scares me little one!'

She looked at him softly. 'How can I prove my trust, my love for you? I will do anything, even if it takes eternity.'

Now they both cried. The tears seemed to cleanse him, he made his decision! 'Then take my hand! You will not leave my side, you must understand, we cannot take on the evil one! We will continue to protect our children and re-unite those souls that come our way!' Even as they spoke, a spirit woman appeared on the sands. She wandered around, calling out her child's name.

'Christina.'

Emma looked up at him. 'I know her.'

Jonathan knew her too, he hesitated. He could not risk losing the child's right to be re-united. 'Go to the mother.' He told Emma. 'I will fetch her daughter to her.' He called to the girl. She caught sight of her mother and screamed with delight. He caught back a sob, 'this is what it was all about!'

It was the beginning of his working alongside his sister. She never left his side, she clucked over his children like a little mother. He could see their faces light up when she approached. Weeks became months, she never failed him. The day came when he let her re-unite a child. Emma had come across a small girl, she lay face down on the sand. She had followed the brother's children down to the water. In life she had been simple of mind. The brother's children had led her to the waters side. Once there, her fate was sealed! They pushed her in! They stood squealing with glee, waiting for her spirit. Somehow, she still lived!

Her little body pulled under then swept by the current onto the sand.

Emma had come running to him. She pulled at his hand. 'Come quickly Jonathan! I have found a child, she is ready to pass!'

They were at the child's side in an instant. They could hear screams of outrage! It was the land children. The girl quivered. All fell silent! It was over! Slowly, her spirit emerged. She stood before them, smiling, Emma held out her hand. He stood back and watched. In the distance, he could see a woman in spirit, she was kin to the girl. Emma looked at him, he nodded. Her smile was his reward as she took the girl to her grandmother. She re-united many more over the months, some new, some old. He got great pleasure watching her. The new spirits, especially the little ones, instinctively went to her.

The year was two thousand. Jonathan was becoming weary. His head was full of questions, when was it going to be `his time`? How would he know? Why had he had no sign? He was doing his patrol of the estate. This, he preferred to do on his own. He looked up at the windows and shuddered. Angry land children glared back at him. He knew the amount of `safe houses` had increased, but many were still without protection. He kept to the perimeter; he had no wish to come across the brothers. Emma's eyes glinted, following him from an upstairs window! At her side were her birth brothers! Unrecognisable! More like horned goats than humans. In the many centuries since the skeletal brothers had taken and hid their spirits, they had become more powerful and evil than they could ever be! They stood at the side of Satan himself! They had the skeletal brothers exiled. Now they put their final plan in place to be rid of Jonathan! Jonathan turned back to the water front. He needed to get away from the oppression of the estate. The evil spirits that roamed there would never be saved, nor did many of them want to be. In life, they had been murderers of the innocents, racists, warmongers! In death, they were demented! They manifested themselves in dreams, turning them into horrific nightmares. Manipulating the young to do horrific crimes. They roamed the streets, seeking revenge on any lost soul. Jonathan hurried to be away. He suddenly stopped. He looked to where the sound of a car being driven at great speed came from. He knew there were a great many being stolen in this area. Before his very eyes, a young boy, still in his school uniform, stood frozen in the road! There was nothing Jonathan could do to save him! The car made no attempt to avoid him. At the wheel was a young boy, his hands gripped tight, his eyes blank! Jonathan's heart jumped! At his side was a land spirit, he urged him on! The schoolboy had no chance! He was hit full on! His body flew through the air! It came down and landed on the bonnet, almost smashing through the windscreen. The car kept going! He was carried along the full length of the road, looking into the faces of his killers. Jonathan kept pace! He could not let them take his soul!

The car slammed its brakes on! The small victim slid to the floor! The driver sat stone faced at the wheel. Jonathan had not quite reached the boy as his spirit left him. He looked around, unsure as to what was happening. Then he caught sight of the evil spirit boy, who held out his hairy hand to him. He pulled away! The evil child growled at his rejection! Jonathan bravely barred his way, he could not show any fear. The child hid behind him, crying for his mummy. The evil one stood his ground. He bared his teeth at Jonathan, who barred his way. People were pouring out of their homes and they ran toward the tragic scene. He did not show fear of Jonathan, he was prepared to do battle! Jonathan knew not to show the sudden terror he felt of this demon, his teeth and claws looked lethal. If he latched onto him, it would then be down to who had the most power! To lose would be fatal for the boy's spirit! Suddenly he saw a flash of fear on the demons face!

He felt someone at his side, it was Emma! The small, rat shaped boy took a step back as Emma pointed at him. Jonathan hardly recognised her voice, it was like a grown woman's, sure! Powerful! 'Be gone, child of Satan! You have lost!' He turned and half ran, half crawled, without looking back. He felt repulsion as it scurried, like a spider, up the back wall of a house before disappearing through a bedroom window.

There were crowds around the broken body of the child. An ambulance and police arrived. The driver still sat motionless, staring through the shattered, blood stained screen.

An elderly spirit man walked through the crowd toward the boy. He smiled and held out his arms. The child ran to him, sobbing. 'Granddad I want my mum.' The man lifted him, in a flash, they were gone!

Jonathan sighed, these were the worst! The sudden deaths! How do you tell someone, especially a child, they no longer exist in life?

They walked hand and hand toward the dock in silence. He led her to a sand dune and they sat. He knew she was ready to take over. She was as powerful as him, if not more. Again it was like she knew his thoughts. 'I am not ready yet, we must wait until we are sure.'

He shook his head. 'You are more than ready. The children love and trust you.' He stopped searching for the right words 'It is me, I am not sure. I always thought that when it was my time, there would be a sign, a message!' He faltered.

She took his hand. He felt a surge of power. She smiled. 'Do not be ashamed of your thoughts, I would feel the same if I were you. Centuries of my betrayals cannot be undone in two years.' She stood. 'You are right! I am sure they will send you a sign.'

He felt relief at her understanding. There would be no turning back once he was gone, leaving her with all his responsibilities, His children!

Her brothers sneered. How easy it had been for her to deceive their eldest brother. How they despised him. He had kept their sister from them too long! Now they would put the next part of their evil intent in place. Tomorrow was the eve of the highest tide of all!

All the next day she stayed at his side. The children too, would not leave them. He watched how she listened to them. She loved and comforted them. He smiled, they adored her. Night time approached as they watched the water swell. She sat at his side and said softly. 'Look brother, look how high the water is. Like the one that took us for two centuries.' She kissed his hand. 'I was nearly lost to you forever. I thank you for saving me.'

He felt so proud of her. Things had never been so good; he actually felt there was hope. He spoke to his children, preparing them for when `his time` came to leave them. He saw uncertainty on their faces, he quickly assured them. 'When I am crossed over, I will strive to become a guardian. One day I will come and bring you all with me.' They gathered nearer, wanting to hear more. He pointed to Emma. 'My sister will look after you until then. She will protect you from the brothers and their demons.' They all turned to her, smiling their trust and love at her. She smiled her gratitude at him.

He continued his talk with them, they told stories of their lives `before`. She turned and gave the signal to the `dog` that skulked in the rushes. She wandered to the quayside and stood peering across the water.

Jonathan looked for her; he saw her at the waterside and called to her. 'What is it you see sister?'

She smiled and shrugged. 'I do not know! There seems to be some sort of light on the water.'

He followed her over, the children followed. He looked out and frowned. 'I see only the waves.'

She looked again. 'You are right! It has gone.'

He turned back, then stopped. 'What was that?' He gasped, as he turned back to the water.

She looked puzzled. 'What?' She too turned back to the water.

He strained to hear over the sound of the waves, his eyes opened wide. 'There! Did you not hear?'

She shook her head, she looked concerned. 'What can you hear? Tell me! You are frightening me!'

He stood still, his face shocked! He could not believe she did not hear their mother!

She looked over the waves again. Suddenly, she gasped. 'I see! I see her!'

He was trembling, he held her hand. 'Where? Where? I cannot see!'

She pointed a quivering finger, he looked, he could not see! He heard it again. 'JONATHAN!'

Then, he saw them! His mother holding her baby! His brothers beckoning to him! They hovered on the waves. Emma grabbed his arm. 'I see them! I see them!'

He threw back his head and gave praise to the Lord. 'My family! My brothers!'

Emma burst out crying! The children ran around scared! They did not see or hear anything!

They called again 'JONATHAN!!'

He turned to Emma; he did not know how to tell her it was `his time!`

She choked back her tears. 'I love you, my brother! Do not forget us!'

He looked at the children. They looked scared, it broke his heart. He turned to Emma for help, she understood. She put on a brave smile 'Remember what we talked about! Jonathan is preparing our path to eternal rest.' He thanked God he had spoken to them, prepared them!

His mother called again. 'JONATHAN!' Her voice was urgent. He had to go, NOW!!

Emma urged him on. 'Go brother!! I will see you again in paradise! We will all be together!'

The children clung to Emma, she held them close 'Say goodbye to Jonathan!'

Jonathan looked out, the figures had become faint. He turned back to the children, he needed their approval.

They held Emma's hand and said as one 'Do not forget us!'

He turned to the water, it swelled, He raised his arms, he could not bare to look back as he committed himself to the deep!

At once, as before, he fell into a black, velvet abyss. Then, without warning, he exploded back to the surface! The scene before him tore him apart! His children screaming inside of a circle! They were surrounded by every evil entity on the waterside. They were tearing at them, fighting for their

spirits. Almost at face level, his sister! She held hands with two devils! They shrieked at him! Laughing as he was sucked back under.

....

.....,,,,,